I AM NOT SLEEPY!

Written and Illustrated by:

Markita Staples-Green

I am not sleepy!

Wellll...maybe I'm a LITTLE sleepy.

Do I HAVE to clean up my toys?

That looks like fun!

Let me help.

I don't want to take a bath.

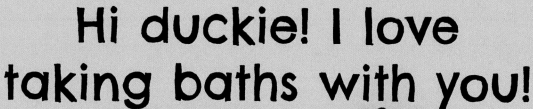

Hi duckie! I love
taking baths with you!

NO

pajamas!

Oooh, I want to wear the soft rainbow ones.

NO! I don't want to brush my teeth!

Look, I can brush all by myself!

No story. I want to jump!

Read that part again please, Mama.

I don't want to wear a bonnet!

I don't want my pretty hair to get messy!

May I have my bonnet, Mama?

Mama come back!
One more kiss, please.

It's too dark, Mama!

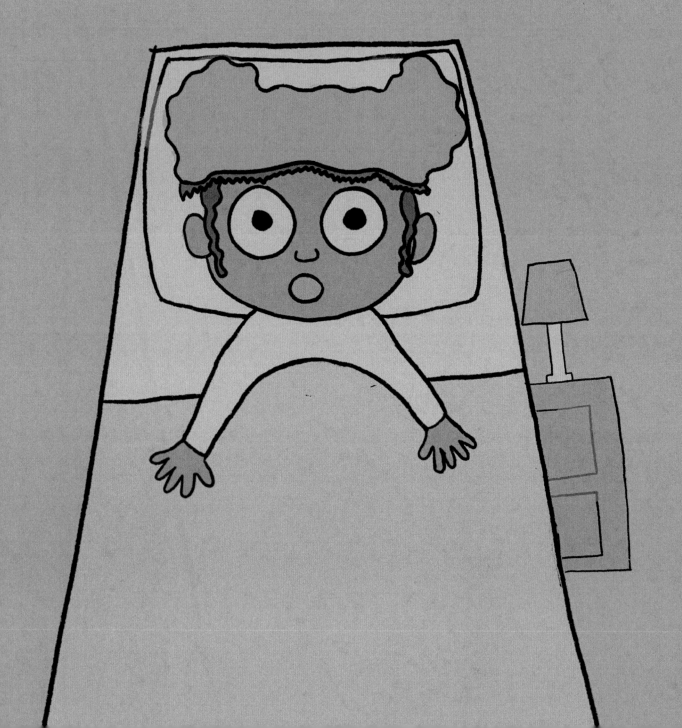

Mmmmm...This is just right.

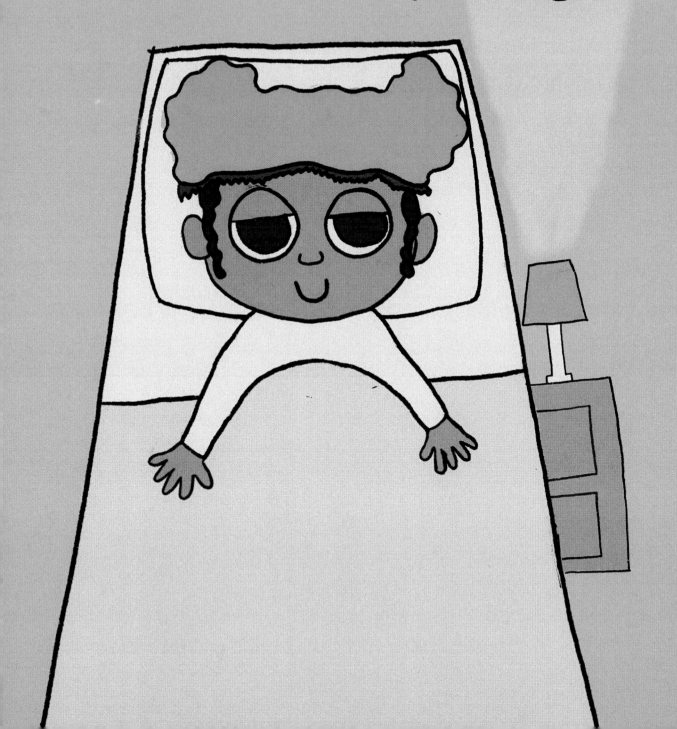

Mama, my baby!

Ahhh. Here she goes.

Good night sweet girl.

Thank you for reading!

Have you read our first book?
Get it on Amazon and the Curly Crew website!

Website & E-mail list: www.curlycrewbooks.com

 @curlycrewbooks

Curly Crew Books

 @curlycrewbooks

Follow the author on   @markiestaples

Made in the USA
Coppell, TX
24 December 2021

69986348R10019